Eliza's Kindergarten Surprise

by Alice B. McGinty

illustrated by Nancy Speir

MARSHALL CAVENDISH CHILDREN

All rights reserved
Marshall Cavendish Corporation, 99 White Plains Road, Tarrytown, New York 10591
www.marshallcavendish.us

Library of Congress Cataloging-in-Publication Data
McGinty, Alice B.
Eliza's kindergarten surprise / by Alice B. McGinty ; illustrated by Nancy Speir. — 1st ed.
p. cm.
Summary: On her first day of school, Eliza fills her pocket with objects—buttons, a pebble, a napkin,
and a piece of yarn—that remind her of her mother, whom she misses very much.
ISBN-13: 978-0-7614-5351-2
[1. First day of school—Fiction. 2. Mother and child—Fiction. 3. Schools—Fiction.] I. Speir, Nancy, ill. II. Title.

PZ7.M16777Eli 2007
[E]—dc22

2006022415

The text of this book is set in Platten Regular.
The illustrations are rendered in acrylic paint on illustration board.

Book design by Becky Terhune

Printed in China

First edition
1 3 5 6 4 2

Marshall Cavendish
Children

To my mom, Linda K. Blumenthal
—A. B. M.

For Ginger
—N. S.

When Mommy walked Eliza to school for her first day of kindergarten, Eliza began to cry. She took a breath and rubbed her eyes. Mommy kissed Eliza warm on her cheeks. She placed a kiss on her fingertips and gently slid it into Eliza's pocket.

"You can carry my kiss in your pocket all day long," Mommy said. "It will be right by your heart. Then, I won't seem so far away."

Eliza's teacher smiled and took Eliza's hand. She led her inside and showed Eliza her very own cubby. She brought her to the circle for morning songs.

ELIZA

J

Eliza sat down in the circle. But her cheeks
felt cold where Mommy's kisses had been,
and her pocket felt empty, too empty inside.

Eliza did not sing morning songs.
She looked down at the rug
instead. There she found
two blue buttons, shiny like
Mommy's shoes.

She held them for a while, rubbed them with her thumbs, then dropped them in her pocket.

During playtime, Eliza peeked inside her
pocket, but even with two blue buttons
shiny like Mommy's shoes, her pocket
felt empty, too empty inside.

Ruth asked Eliza if she wanted to play tag, but Eliza answered sadly, "I don't feel like playing."

She crawled inside a tunnel to hide.

There she found a
pebble, smooth and
bright like Mommy's skin.

She held it for a while, pressed it warm on her cheeks, then dropped it in her pocket.

At snack time, Eliza didn't feel like eating. She poked at her crackers and looked down at her napkin.

The napkin was bumpy and red like Mommy's dress.

Eliza put it in her pocket, too.

During arts and crafts, Eliza peeked inside her pocket again.

But even with two blue buttons, a smooth
bright pebble, and a bumpy red napkin,

her pocket felt empty, too empty inside.

"I want my Mommy!" Eliza said.

She pushed away the markers and the clothespin, the paste and the yarn that were on the table for making a scarecrow.

That's when Eliza saw the piece of yarn was the same color as Mommy's golden brown hair. She dropped it in her pocket and peeked inside.

There she saw the two blue buttons,
shiny like Mommy's shoes,

the pebble, smooth and bright
like Mommy's skin,

the napkin, bumpy and red
like Mommy's dress,

and the piece of golden yarn,
the color of Mommy's hair.

When Eliza saw everything
together, she knew just
what to do.

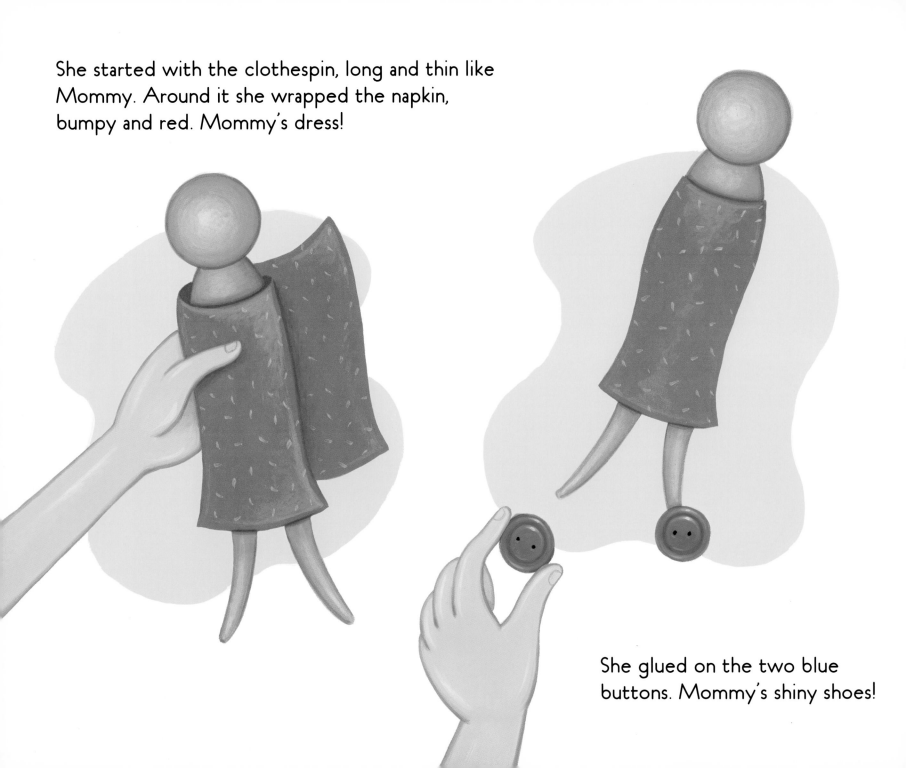

She started with the clothespin, long and thin like Mommy. Around it she wrapped the napkin, bumpy and red. Mommy's dress!

She glued on the two blue buttons. Mommy's shiny shoes!

Then, out of her pocket she took the smooth bright pebble and the golden yarn. She glued the yarn to the pebble and the pebble to the clothespin. They became Mommy's head, with golden brown hair.

She gave Mommy warm green eyes and a big red smile, too.

"Look," said Eliza to her teacher. "I have a surprise. It's Mommy!" She gave Mommy a kiss and slid her into her pocket.

"I can put Mommy in my pocket," Eliza said with a smile. "She'll be right by my heart, and I'll carry her with me all day long."

During music, Eliza and Mommy sang every song.

When it was time for recess, Eliza and Ruth and Mommy *all* played tag.

Before she knew it, it was time to go home. Eliza looked up and saw . . .

Mommy!

"I have a surprise for you," Eliza said. "Guess who's in my pocket?" Mommy leaned down and looked closely at the smooth, bright pebble with the golden-brown hair. She touched the bumpy red dress and the shiny blue shoes.

"Me?" she asked.
Eliza nodded.

Mommy smiled and reached into her own pocket.

"I have a surprise for you, too," she said. "Guess who is in *my* pocket?"

"Me?" Eliza asked.

Mommy nodded. "I missed you, too."

Eliza gently slid her hand into Mommy's.

"It's a good thing pockets can hold so much!" Eliza said.